E Lan
c.1
Langdo, Bryan.

The dog who loved the
good life /
2001.   2-02

P9-DCN-930

HA CASS COUNTY PUBLIC LIBRARY
400 E. MECHANIC
HARRISONVILLE, MO 64701

THE DOG WHO LOVED THE GOOD LIFE

Bryan Langdo

Henry Holt and Company   •   New York

0 0022 0231446 0

HA   CASS COUNTY PUBLIC LIBRARY
400 E. MECHANIC
HARRISONVILLE, MO 64701

Henry Holt and Company, LLC
Publishers since 1866
115 West 18th Street
New York, New York 10011

Henry Holt is a registered trademark of Henry Holt and Company, LLC
Copyright © 2001 by Bryan Langdo
All rights reserved.
Published in Canada by Fitzhenry & Whiteside Ltd.,
195 Allstate Parkway, Markham, Ontario L3R 4T8.

Library of Congress Cataloging-in-Publication Data
Langdo, Bryan.
The dog who loved the good life / by Bryan Langdo.
Summary: Mr. Hibble's new dog, Jake, is very cute and cuddly, but he likes to
do human things—such as eating at the dinner table and brushing his teeth.
[1. Dogs—Fiction.] I. Title.
PZ7.L2575Do 2001 [E]—dc21 00-57530

ISBN 0-8050-6494-X / Designed by Martha Rago / First Edition—2001
The artist used Winsor & Newton watercolors on Aquarelle
Arches paper to create the illustrations for this book.
Printed in the United States of America on acid-free paper. ∞
1 3 5 7 9 10 8 6 4 2

For my mom and dad,
for always being there

Mr. Hibble loved his new dog, Jake. Jake was small. He was furry. He had lots of personality.

But Jake wanted more than a bowl of puppy chow on the floor.

Jake expected to eat dinner at the table.

He used Mr. Hibble's toothbrush at bedtime.
Mr. Hibble was a bit surprised at this behavior,
but maybe the dog just needed to be trained.

Jake was in the cozy chair when Mr. Hibble wanted to watch his favorite detective show. This was Mr. Hibble's chance to start training his dog.

"Get down," he said, firmly and clearly. Jake just turned on cartoons.

When Mr. Hibble went to visit his niece, Sara, he brought Jake along. They were all playing in the yard when the neighbor's dog walked by.

"If I had a dog, I'd dress him up just like that," Sara said. "And then we'd have a tea party!"

Jake laughed. Mr. Hibble sighed.

Jake even tagged along when Mr. Hibble
met his friend Miss Crabble for dinner. He
didn't want to miss all the fun.

He was not invited, and Miss Crabble
didn't like dogs, but Jake made himself
right at home.

One day
Mr. Hibble's car
keys were missing.

He looked
all over, but they
were nowhere
to be found.

Strangely, neither
was Jake.

Mr. Hibble finally had to take the bus to work.

When Mr. Hibble came home that night and saw the mess, he was very upset. Where had all the food come from? Who were all these *dogs*?

Mr. Hibble had had enough.

"That's it, Jake!" said Mr. Hibble.
"You're sleeping in the doghouse tonight!"

But Jake didn't want to stay in the doghouse. It didn't have heat or hot water—or a television.

Mr. Hibble's house was much nicer.
Jake pressed his nose against the window
longingly.

Then he had an idea. What if Mr. Hibble didn't see him come in?

It sure felt good to be home again!

Jake got ready for bed.
"Jake!" shouted a surprised Mr. Hibble.
"How did you get in?"

The next morning Mr. Hibble put Jake
on a bus to California.

That dog wants the good life, he thought. Well, he'll love a nice vacation! Mr. Hibble waved good-bye.

A few days later a huge phone bill
came in the mail. Mr. Hibble wondered who
had made all those expensive calls.

In walked Jake, wearing his owner's
best underwear.
"What on earth!" exclaimed Mr. Hibble.
"How did you get back?"

Mr. Hibble was stumped. "What am I going to do about Jake?" he asked himself.

All kinds of possibilities
went through his mind.

Then Mr. Hibble thought of the perfect
solution. Sara loved dogs. Jake loved
being pampered. The two of them would
get along wonderfully.

From that day on, Sara always had someone to play with.

Mr. Hibble finally had some peace and quiet.

And Jake got to sit at the table.